T0380374

LOVE
IS
ALL
AROUND:

A COLLECTION OF
SHORT STORIES

GRANT LITTON

Copyright © 2021 by Grant Litton. 830186

All rights reserved. No part of this book may
be reproduced or transmitted in any form or by
any means, electronic or mechanical, including
photocopying, recording, or by any information storage
and retrieval system, without permission in writing
from the copyright owner.

This is a work of fiction. Names, characters, places
and incidents either are the product of the author's
imagination or are used fictitiously, and any
resemblance to any actual persons, living or dead,
events, or locales is entirely coincidental.

To order additional copies of this book, contact:
Xlibris
844-714-8691
www.Xlibris.com
Orders@Xlibris.com

ISBN: Softcover   978-1-6641-7379-8
        EBook   978-1-6641-7378-1

Print information available on the last page

Rev. date: 05/06/2021

LOVE
IS
ALL
AROUND:

A COLLECTION OF
SHORT STORIES

CONTENTS

An Angel At The Dinner Table

CHAPTER 1

As the alarm clock rings, Jessie rolls over groggily and smacks at the small beeping box until it goes silent when she knocks it off the nightstand. She groans, rubbing her foggy green eyes as she sits up and scratches her head through her long blonde hair as she tries to come alive. She stands up and staggers across the room in her worn cheer shirt from HS as she grabs a towel and heads across the hall for the shower. She slowly takes the tattered shirt off and tosses it in the bathroom floor as she kicks off her flowered cotton panties as she steps in the shower, turning on the water. As she feels the steaming water flood over her fit body, she starts to come alive, wondering what the day, and her job will bring today.

She steps out of the shower and dries off, wrapping the fluffy blue towel around her, as she brushes her teeth and runs a brush through her hair before running back across the hall to throw on her work uniform for the day. She runs downstairs and finds her folks sitting at the dining room table finishing breakfast before they go off to work. "Hey, don't forget, we're going out of town for a meeting, we'll be back tomorrow evening sometime. There's food in the fridge." The young lady grabs a couple pop tarts and fills her metal cup with milk, kisses them both and runs out the door, as she hops in her car to make the short drive to her job at the local diner.

The car pulls in the back of the diner, music blaring as she gets out and locks her car, busting through the door while greeting the other girls as well as her surly boss who definitely isn't a morning person. About 10 mins into her shift as she's working on the place settings, she hears one of the girls saying that someone sat in her section, so she grabs her notepad and walks out, where she sees a nice-looking older man looking over the menu. "Hi honey, I'm Jessie and I'll be your server today, can I start ya off with a drink?" Without even looking up, he says "uhhh milk's fine, thanks..." She walks to the back to get his milk as he looks up, he inadvertently catches a look at her walking away, noticing her hips swaying in the uniform but goes back to looking over the food. When she comes back, he looks at her, "Hey Jessie, my name's Paul. So, how's the humongo platter?" as she looks down at him with a bit of a shocked look on her face, you sure you want that sir? No one's finished it yet. He looks up at her assuredly "I'm a construction worker, we've got that job over on Gibb St. "Oh ok…. well yeah, you probably need some food in ya," with a wink "one humongo comin' up honey!" before walking away. As she walks to the back, she thinks about the sweet burly guy sitting in her section, the way his eyes sparkle… his freshly groomed moustache…as she thinks to herself "he probably doesn't even notice me." After about 5 mins she brings out his massive platter of food and sets it down in front of him. "Wow, thanks…. that looks perfect!" He proceeds to tackle the massive platter of bacon, biscuits and gravy, sausage, and fruit, as she brings his bill to the table. "Whenever you're ready, I'll come pick it up" with a smile, and she walks away again. After getting his fill, he leaves the money for the meal with a hefty tip on the table and walks out the door.

CHAPTER 2

Over the next few weeks, he returns to the diner for his new go-to meal and his favorite server, hoping he isn't being creepy. One day he's there for his daily calorie overload, after which he needs to go across the street to pick something up at the store. When he comes back from the store, he hears some kind of commotion, he looks around, finally walking around the back of the diner, he sees Jessie arguing with some guy as he pushes her against the car. Without hesitation, he runs up, spins the guy around and decks him, kicking him in the ribs once for good measure. "You know that idiot?!" "Yeah... my ex...." She says, as she wipes a tear from her eye, her makeup smeared. He pulls a tissue out of his pocket and dabs her eyes. Can I take you somewhere? She looks up at him slightly embarrassed how she must look, "No...I wouldn't wanna intrude..." He scoffs gently, "Hey... my momma taught me right, so when a lady needs help, I do what I can!" As he walks her to his truck and helps her in, he starts up the truck and goes in to tell someone what happened, and that she had to leave. As he gets in the truck, he thinks briefly before driving off in the other direction from her house. "Uh...where are we going? I live back the other way..." she says, with a puzzled look on her face. The sweet man looks at her, "well you said that was your ex, right?" "yeah...?" "Well... he knows where you live, unless you moved recently... and he probably won't be too happy that I may have broken his jaw..." Besides, I've got a spare room if you need to relax or anything else you need... it's just me and Lucy." She thinks to herself, "great...I meet this cute guy, and he's gonna take me home to hang out with his wife.... I'm in so much trouble!" As they pull up to a small unassuming house, she gets out of the truck and looks at him; "So...uhhh, who's Lucy?" As she finishes asking her question, he opens the door, and the most adorable little bulldog comes out running back and forth around her legs. "Get down Lucy!" "Aww... she's so adorable..." she slowly bends down and plays with the overactive pup then walks into the small house, looking around as he flips through some mail. "The spare room's down the hall on the right... The bathroom's on the left about halfway down if you need it."

CHAPTER 3

She looks at the stranger, "I…I don't know what to say…. you didn't have to do this…. I must look a mess…." he just kinda chuckles, eh, nothin' a few touch-ups with make-up and some clean clothes won't fix." She laughs nervously, "yeah. I guess you're right…but I don't have anything with me." He gets up and starts walking down the hall, coming back out with an old football jersey and some shorts." I dunno if they'll fit, but you're welcome to them. The phone's over by the kitchen if you need to call your house and let them know what's going on." "Crap!" she thinks… they're gone till tomorrow, and I'm all alone with this stranger." "Uhhh… it's ok… I'll worry about it later" as she shuffles nervously, before walking down the hall to the bathroom, she shuts the door and strips down, slipping into his shower, turning on the blazing water." As she feels the water wash over her toned frame, she thinks about the day she's had… from dealing with unruly customers to the fight in the parking lot to being naked in a stranger's house after just a couple of weeks."

After a revitalizing shower, she slips the jersey on, but the shorts are too big. She thinks to herself "well, the shirt's pretty long and he's been a gent so far, maybe he won't even notice" as she leaves the shorts in the bathroom floor, putting on some basic makeup she walks back out. He's flipping through the channels, hearing her come in but not seeing her. "There… feel better?" she takes a deep breath "Yeah, thanks…" as she nervously walks in front of the couch and sits down on the opposite side, giving him the first indication that she doesn't look like she's wearing the shorts, he stifles a breath as Lucy comes up and sits between them on the couch, her head on the young girl's leg.

CHAPTER 4

Thank you again…you didn't have to do this." As he looks over at her, trying not to look over her amazing frame; "Like I said, just doing what every guy should do when a girl's in trouble, they taught me that in the service! ""oh…...you served…? Well, I guess now I have two reasons to thank you!" Well not much to me really… I pretty much keep to myself… I cheered in school, now I'm sitting out before going to community college in the spring: I wanna become a masseuse. Suddenly he looks at her with a goofy smile…. that's pretty awesome… maybe when you finish school, I can hire ya for my personal masseuse. All those years in the military, my back's a mess." She looks over at him nervously… "Do…do you want me to work on your back? Free of course… to make up for you helping me out." Suddenly he slowly slides away from the back of the couch and turns slightly towards her, as she takes his cue and crawls behind him as he starts to feel her petite hands working on his neck muscles, putting her thumbs down both sides before going out to his massive shoulders, rubbing them as thoroughly as she can.

Next, he feels her run her small palms up and down his chiseled back muscles just off his spine, rolling her knuckles in different spots to work out some knots as he lets out a slight purr of excitement, biting his lip as he realizes he did it out loud. "Do you have enough room back there, or should I lay on the floor?" Oh uhhh… you sure it's ok, I don't wanna make it worse by having you on the floor." without hesitation, he takes his shirt the rest of the way off, putting his amazing chiseled/scarred back on display and lays down on the floor.

As she goes back to working over his muscular back, he feels her working on specific spot. "Everything ok back there?" grunting as she tries to work on a knot "Uhhh yeah…. hey uhhh…. do… do you mind if I straddle your back to get more pressure on this one spot?" Out of her view, he bites his lip; "well…if… if you think that'll help…" Forgetting that she wasn't wearing the borrowed gym shorts, she stands up, steps over his back, and sits down nervously on the small of his back, the feel of her skinny butt pressing against his back with just the cotton material between them sends a chill through his body, as she starts working over it again. Lost in the moment as her tiny hands work their magic, he starts moaning lightly. Hearing him making the noises, not only makes her feel like she's doing something right with the massage, but suddenly she can feel herself getting slightly turned on, her fluid starting to leak out of her bald virgin pussy.

CHAPTER 5

After what feels forever, she takes a break, and he snaps out of a trance......." wow.... that was amazing..." Without thinking, he rolls over, but instead of falling to the side, suddenly they find themselves staring eye to eye as she sits on his muscular torso looking slightly flushed... "I......I'm sorry... I should've...." Suddenly she starts to lean down before snapping out of it and realizing what she was doing.... he looks up at her." Forgive me for being direct but have you....... ever been with a guy like this...?" biting his lip nervously, trying not to overreact and freak out his young friend. "Uhhh...n... no...should I... should I get up?" Seeing her turn beet red, he looks up at her "I don't know what's on your mind, but I want you to know I wouldn't do anything you weren't comfy with...." as he bites his lip nervously, suddenly she starts leaning back down towards him and before she knows it, she feels his warm wet tongue sloshing in her mouth, as she tries to mimic his moves awkwardly. As he breaks the kiss, she sits there with her eyes still closed "......that......that was amazing...." She opens her eyes, looking up into his crystal blue eyes, he notices them looking down a t the jersey, then nervously back to her face...." Do...do you want me to take it off Paul?" biting her lip in anticipation that this might actually be happening for her. "Only... only if you want to..." suddenly she grabs the shirt tail and starts to lift it, as he grabs his huge hands around her ribs, so she doesn't lose her balance as she slides the tee off and tosses it nervously on the floor. He sits there in shock as the shirt comes off showing off her perky white breasts with puffy pinkish nipples, a flat tummy with a belly ring and the cotton panties that have been on his back during the massage.

Seeing the look on his face, she starts to frown. "You...you don't like it do you? She says disappointedly "No.... that's not it at all...you look amazing, I just didn't want to do anything to make you uncomfortable......Can...Can I...touch your breasts? Have you ever been touched?" She looks up at him, showing a slightly more relaxed face that he thought she was pretty, but nervous for being touched for the first time. "I... I've never done anything with a guy... but yes.... if you want to touch them....... just be gentle...." Suddenly she feels Paul's large hands sliding up her flat tummy, he plays with her belly ring for a moment before running his huge hands over her slightly larger than average pale breasts gently. She closes her eyes, lost in the moment as he rubs her soft, tender mounds gently, he runs his index finger over her puffy pink nipples, causing them to poke out excitedly as she tries to stifle a moan of excitement. Seeing her biting her lip in excitement, he looks at her face, "Do….do you trust me…?" keeping her eyes closed, biting her lip, she just nods. Suddenly he pulls her closer, kissing her deeply, but this time he runs his tongue down her neck and before she knows what's going on, she feels him licking and sucking on her breasts gently, tugging her pink nips with his teeth, as she lets out a squeak of approval. As he buries his face in her mounds, she runs her fingers through his thick brown hair.

After a few mins he pulls back out as she looks at him with a pensive look. "Is everything ok?" She stammers momentarily before gaining some courage. "Can... can I... take your pants off?" as her face turns blood red, he looks up at her. "Sit …back on the couch…" she does as she's was told, and he stands up in front her "So... you've never done any of this?" she worriedly shakes her head "no" still looking up into his crystal blue eyes. "Unbutton and unzip them…" she looks down at the button and back up at him as he nods his head in approval; she nervously unbuttons his jeans as the button pops out, she jumps slightly before unzipping him, seeing his tighty whities with a huge bulge peeking out as she bites her lip… "Are you ready to pull them down?" he asks, as suddenly she takes a deep breath, nodding nervously, she wiggles them down his muscular legs, seeing his full tighty whities, but her eyes still locked on the amazing bulge."

CHAPTER 6

As he sees the shock in her face, he looks into her green eyes; Do you want me to take your panties off now or do you want to?" she looks at him with a frightened look of excitement; "you...you can…" Suddenly, he grabs under her arms and stands her up off the couch, locking eyes "are you ready?" she waits for a second, taking a deep breath, she nods as she feels him slip her damp panties down off her long tan legs, feeling the air on her bald virgin pussy gently, as he looks over her now nude body, she steps out of the panties wadded on the floor, standing there swaying awkwardly. You…....you look amazing….do….do you……... explore?" as she looks puzzled, she nods her head 'no." As they maintain eye contact, she feels his hand on her flat tummy again, this time, she tenses up nervously as she feels him slide his hand downward, tracing a circle around her puffy wet pussy slowly. Next, she bites her lip as she feels nerve impulses shoot through her body as he rubs up and down over her hood. "Ohhh…oh my..." she wiggles around in excitement, but as she moves around, it causes him to split her velvety soft lips with two fingers, as he slowly moves them back and forth before giving her a 'come here' motion from the inside, as feels her inner walls." "oh…oh my…that…oh…

Without even asking, he takes her tiny hand, slowly he slips it inside his waistband, as she feels something that feels like a kielbasa. "Is… is that your…OMG it's so big…are they all that big?!" he chuckles nervously, "no…. just lucky I guess……. you ready to see it?" she swallows a lump in her throat, and nods anxiously. As he slips his fingers out of her wet spot, he slides his tighty whities off as suddenly his solid 9 inches flops out in front of her as her eyes go wide." OH… OH MY…" she's so excited for what she sees that she reaches out to grab it without even asking, causing him to tense up. "E…Easy… don't squeeze so hard… rub it slowly…

CHAPTER 7

He can't help but let out an audible moan as her tiny hands work over his massive member like she's been doing it for years. He grabs on to her shoulders as his knees quiver at the feeling of the nerves in his legs tingling at her feeling. "Do… Do you want me to… taste you?" as he looks nervously into her green eyes. Suddenly she stops stroking his member and looks into his sparkling eyes with anticipation. "Are…. are you sure you want to?" as she bites her lip, only hearing her friends talk about how it feels to be eaten out. He steps back from her nude body, "…...lay in the floor... unless you'd rather go down the hall." nervously he reaffirms with her "If…if you don't want to do it, I won't… just tell me to stop." She nervously takes his hand as they walk down the hall to her guest room as she lays down flat on the bed, looking up at the designs in the plaster on the ceiling.

He crawls up on the bed and kisses her deeply, again, running his tongue down her body. He circles her tender mounds, down her flat tummy, tugs her belly ring with his teeth, and suddenly he stops, hovering over her bald soaked pussy, his warm breath causing chill bumps to form on her skin. He takes a deep breath, then leans down and starts licking around the wet puffy mound, tasting her fluid, hearing her start to moan slightly. Next, he moves closer to the middle, sliding his warm wet tongue gently over her soft lips, as she starts to massage his head through his dark brown hair, she feels him slip his tongue inside her wet spot, her body tingling all over at the feeling as he traces her inner rim slowly.

As she keeps massaging the back of his head, her heart racing, he slowly reaches underneath her, grabbing her butt briskly, pulling her deeper onto his tongue as she shrieks in excitement, having never felt anything like this before. As he continues to grind into her, just on instinct, she pulls her long legs over his muscular back, which plunges him so deep inside her that she feels like his tongue will come out the other side. 'OH…OH MY…OMG…. HOLY…OH THAT'S AMAZING...OH YES…" Her words fueling his confidence, he grinds harder and faster inside her until she feels like she wants to explode! Finally, after what seems like forever, he pulls out of her, sliding up her nude body, he kisses her again, allowing her to taste her own fluid on his tongue.

She looks into his sparkling eyes, "can... can I taste you too?" as she blushes nervously, never thinking she'd ask a guy that, let alone someone she just met recently! He pauses before rolling over on the bed, his member standing at attention, she nervously grabs it and stares at it before licking the tip like a popsicle. As he feels her tongue rub his tip, he tenses up, grabbing the bed to keep him from flying up from the amazing feeling! She feels a bit more confident, seeing his reaction, she starts licking lower around his shaft before putting most of his swollen member inside her mouth and running her lips back and forth over it a few times, hoping she's doing it right.

As he lays there staring up at the light, feeling nerve impulses shoot through his body like a Midwest thunderstorm, he runs his long strong fingers through her blonde hair. OH Yes...That's amazing Jessie....... you sure you've never done this?! OH ...OH MY... F....

CHAPTER 8

He feels the pressure building up between his legs, but finally she sits up and catches her breath. "Did...did I really do good Paul?" He looks up into her green eyes, "You were amazing honey... so...sh......should we....... you know...? She gets a smile on her face from his validation before hearing his suggestion. "Will...will it hurt?" He reassuringly rubs her hips slowly, "only......only when we finish, but the buildup will be amazing......I hope you know I'd never hurt you...." A smile comes back to her face as she looks at her nude friend in front of her on the bed...still not believing the last hour.

I......I would be honored to have you as my first....... you've been nothing but a gentleman, as she bites her lip nervously. He suddenly grabs her by the waist and pulls her over on top of him, lining up their sweaty nude bodies, he nervously reaches down and slips his swollen member inside her tight virgin pussy, just trying to start a rhythm without hurting or scaring his young friend. She gasps in pleasure, feeling it split her soft pale lips slowly, as she wraps her hands around his torso, locking her fingers around the small of his back, her fingertips barely touching his solid muscular butt. He slowly starts going harder and faster, as she moans in pleasure with each thrust.

CHAPTER 9

As he keeps pounding back and forth inside his young friend, he maintains eye contact with her to see the pleasure in her eyes as she bites her lip, trying to stifle a moan of pleasure as she bounces up and down on his amazing member. As he continues to thrust back and forth, going harder and faster, she finally loses control and lets out a moan or two in ecstasy, slightly embarrassed to make an audible noise, but frankly right now she doesn't care! Oh…oh that…. that feels amazing! Suddenly she sits up, she starts grinding back and forth on him, sending a chill through her body with each thrust of his sweaty member rubbing against her velvety soft lips. OH…OH YES! He slowly runs his massive, calloused hands over her legs slowly as he moves his hands behind her, grabbing her butt briskly, as he massages it

During the next few minutes, she starts gaining more confidence as she wiggles around, rolling over, now on top of him. She starts bouncing harder and faster on his member, slightly surprising him at her newfound gusto. He grabs the rails of the headboard as he slightly thrusts his hips upward as she bounces, their meeting causing extra pleasure for both of them as he grunts each time she slams against him, her amazing soft breasts bouncing all over the place, he finally reaches up to massage them to keep them from getting to out of control as he pinches her nips playfully. Suddenly after what feels like forever, he looks down with a weird look then looks back up at her. "Is… Is everything ok?" she asks nervously, wondering if she did something wrong. "I… I think I'm about to…should I pull out?" he asks nervously, not wanting to force anything on his wonderful friend. Suddenly she thinks to herself, "OMG, this is it……! I'm finally gonna be a woman and my friends won't tease me anymore…but will it hurt…? Guess there's one way to find out…" finally she looks up at him with an apprehensive look, "yes… let's go for it… I trust you!"

Hearing her give her consent, he slowly reaches down and grabs her butt again, as he almost goes into a trance-like state, he slams into her, harder and faster as she screams in pleasure while her body slaps against his. "OH… OH YES…OH MY GOD… OH…OH…" Suddenly, her feelings of pleasure are met with a flood of his goo blasting inside her body, as her walls tear and she feels his member break down the walls of her virginity as she lets out a gasp, having never felt such a feeling! Feeling his member shoot into her like a firehose trying to put out a fire, he collapses back on the bed in exhaustion, looking up at the pattern of the plaster on the ceiling. You……. you were… amazing! Did… did you like it? Still sweating and panting from her workout, blushing at his question……." I…I loved it… did…did I really do a good job?" He looks up at her sweaty, slightly embarrassed face with a smile, seeing a twinkle in her eye. "Yes… you were perfect… So how does it feel to not be a virgin anymore?" she looks down at him so touched by how special he's made her feel. "Thank you….it was all I've ever dreamed about…"

CHAPTER 10

He slides out of her as she lays on the bed beside him, she notices his messy goo covering his dick. With a smile, she reaches over and strokes the messy staff, her fingers all sticky, she licks her fingers with a shy smile and laughs as she crawls back up and lays beside her new special friend. They lay there in the bed for another hour or so, just talking about life, then she gets up and walks through the house to make some dinner for them. "What will I tell my parents when they get home?" she wonders. "Ehhh…. they don't have to know just yet."

Smelling something heavenly, he walks down the hall, meeting his friend cooking in the kitchen wearing just a smile as he walks up behind her and smacks her butt playfully. "That smells amazing!" she turns her head around and kisses hm "It's the least I could do for mew new favorite person." With a wink. She looks at him, "you know I'm gonna have to go back home soon… my parents will be home this evening and will wonder where I've been if I'm not there." He sighs and says to her "well, ok, as long as we can keep seeing each other. No one has to know yet." She finishes cooking dinner, as he eats the amazing food, she goes down the hall and gets dressed, collecting some things in a bag to get ready to go home as she sits on the couch. After about an hour, he gets a shower and gets some clothes on so he can take her back to the restaurant to get her car so she can go back to her normal life.

SAFETY IN THE UNKNOWN

CHAPTER 1

"Let's go! Let's go ladies!" yells the surly coach as volleyball practice goes into the last stretch before closing up for the day, Megan changes shoes and packs them in her bag and starts to walk home. A few blocks away, she's walking down a street when a random thug jumps out trying to take her bag. She struggles with him and just as she gets knocked to the ground, she sees a blur and the thug hits the ground! She looks up and sees a nice guy standing there with his fists up…." Th… thank you…" as he reaches out a hand to help her up, she shakily dusts herself off as he hands her the bag. Are you ok? Can I help you get somewhere?" she takes a second to compose herself I…I was just going home, you're more than welcome to walk with me," blushing nervously.

As they walk down the small-town street making small talk, "hey, I'm Donnie, nice to meet you… wish it could've been under better circumstances." She looks nervously at him, still shaking slightly, "uhhh yeah. …. I'm Megan, thanks again…" over the next few minutes she learns that he just moved to town recently and is in the next grade up. As they walk up to a small house, she stops and looks at him. "Well, this is me… thanks again!" As he starts to walk away, she calls out to him…" Uhh hey… you wanna come in for a bite to eat or something to drink?" he blushes slightly, "oh…. I…I wouldn't wanna get you I in trouble with your folks or your…boyfriend…" She chuckles, "it's just me for a few hours, and don't worry, no boyfriend here…c'mon in!" As he thinks it over, he nervously walks into the house, looking around he sits on a fluffy white couch as she listens to the answering machine.

CHAPTER 2

"Can I get you a drink? A snack? It's the least I could do for saving my life…" he chuckles nervously, a coke is fine." She comes back with a glass of ice and a coke as he looks at her, "hey, I got an idea…you've had hella day, why don't you go get a nice warm shower and I can whip you up something to eat…?" she thinks about his offer, knowing that he's way too generous, but after being almost robbed, she could use a hot shower! "Well ok…as long as I'm not putting you out…" with a chuckle, he starts walking to her kitchen, "c'mon, get goin'!" The young lady walks up to the bathroom and hops in the shower, thinking about her day…from class, to practice, meeting her guardian angel, lost in the moment, suddenly she remembers that she forgot her change of clothes. She frantically, tries to decide if she'll grab her towel and take a run for it, or if she'll ask for help.

After about a half hour, she yells for her newfound savior. "Uhhh…hey Donnie… can you help me?" he stops for a minute, hearing her voice, he nervously runs down the hall outside the bathroom door. "Is everything ok?" still embarrassed at her mistake, "Uhh…yeah…but uhhh…could you do me a favor? I got so excited about a hot shower, I didn't grab any clothes… can you go to my room and grab me a few things?" Biting his lip at her request, "Uhh…. sure… anything in particular?" "No," she adds nervously, as he walks into the pastel covered room with volleyball trophies all over the walls. He walks up to a nightstand as he opens the drawer to a stack of gym shorts and old tees, and he picks out a pair of black shorts and a faded shirt from an old volleyball tournament. A few drawers down, he opens up to find a collection of cotton panties and silky thongs, he nervously grabs a thong, looking at it. "Nahh… that'd just be creepy…" he thinks to himself, as he grabs a plain pair of purple bikinis and a matching bra, he nervously walks back to the bathroom door.

CHAPTER 3

"So uhhh.... you want me to just leave them in front of the door or what?" from the other side of the door, she says "if you can crack the door and put them on the sink, that'd be fine..." he takes a deep breath and cracks the door open, just enough to slide his hand in with the clothing pile. Suddenly he notices her reflection in the bathroom mirror, showing off her amazing backside peeking out of the shower curtain as he nervously shuts the door. "I'm going back to finish up dinner, when you're done getting ready, it should be fixed."

He runs back to the kitchen to finish the meal, trying not to focus on his sneak peek of his newfound friend as she comes downstairs in the shorts and tee. "Did I pick good?" he chuckles as she gives him a compliment with a joking tone. Suddenly she gets a whiff of something amazing..." What is that it smells incredible!" I hope you like chicken pasta alfredo, it was my momma's recipe. She sits down as he brings her a coke and a steaming plate of the fragrant noodles as he sits down across from her at the table as she takes a bite. "OMG this is so good! I don't know many guys that can cook like this!" He blushes at her compliment as they make more small talk over the amazing food. She looks up at him, "I wish there was some way I could repay you for this...all of it... the food...saving my life...your... girlfriend must be really proud to have a guy like you!" suddenly, the smile leaves his face. "She.... she cheated on me last week..." she looks at him with a sad look, "Oh...I.... I'm sorry I shouldn't have said anything like that..." he looks at her, "it's ok...you didn't know....

She looks at him and smiles, "hey, you wanna go swimming?" Suddenly he looks at her surprised, "I mean…. yeah, it'd be nice, but…we can't…" she looks at him with a weird look "well why not, it's just out on the patio out there...." blushing, he stammers, "well uhhh…....for one, you just got a nice warm shower... and I don't have any trunks." She chuckles "you…you mean you've never gone skinny dippin' ?" as she smiles shyly. Totally flustered, he looks at her nervously, thinking about the mirror, 'N…no… have you?" She looks at her hero and thinks for a second, "No, but I've always wanted to try it…." Not realizing he's turning beet red, "Well uhhh… I…I guess we'll be in the water, right… and I'd give you the privacy you needed to get in…"

CHAPTER 4

She grabs his hand and slowly walks him out to the patio deck, as she dips her toe in the water, "mmm... feels good..." as she starts to lift her shirt, he nervously turns around quickly." He tenses up when he hears her give an excited scream and splashes into the water, he nervously turns around to see her swimming with the water lapping against her tan skin, just below the split of her chest. He suddenly gives her a hand motion to turn around, as she does, he takes a deep breath and strips down and hops in the water. He surfaces a few feet away from her as he looks at her, trying not to look at her torso. "So uhhh…what do we do now?" She laughs at him, "well silly, we swim!" suddenly she swims towards the deep end, her amazing butt shining from the sun on her wet skin."

She watches from the deep end as he tries swimming towards her, making sure everything stays down in the water, as she laughs at him. "Are you ok? You seem nervous about something…" he looks at her biting his lip, "can…can I make a confession…?" she nods "of course…" as he spits out some water that splashed in his mouth, "well Uhh... I... I've never... been with a beautiful lady…" as his face turns red. "Aww you're adorable…well I've never done anything like this with a hot guy, so there!" she smiles shyly before swimming to him, stopping barely a foot from his nude body. "You…you wanna do more than swim don't you…" her face lights up…" oh darn…you caught me… but hey, I'm 18 so it's not like it's anything wrong," as she smiles softly, her green eyes sparkling with her mid length red hair slicked back from the water.

CHAPTER 5

As he looks over her beautiful face, "uhhh…so…. have…. have you had any…you know… "experiences?" or still a good girl?" she blushes back at him, "well…I've kissed a guy, but that's it, pretty sad for bein' 19 right?... you?" He blushes, looking back at her, "uhhh same….so Uhh…. what you wanna do?" As she looks at her friend, seeing how nervous he must be, "so you've never seen a girl's body before?" he swallows a lump in his throat" well uhhh…. like, my little cousins or other babies, but uhhh…. not like this…." *she swims to the shallower end, turning around to him towards the deep end, "come down to this end…" she watches as he swims closer, more of his chiseled torso comes up out of the water, suddenly she starts walking backwards towards the shallow end, as suddenly her amazing D cups come into view out of the water with water dropping off of her dark red nipples as he stands there in shock. "Do you like what you see?" as she smiles shyly, all he can do is nod. "Do….do you want to…touch them?" he nervously shuffles closer to her as he stands about a foot away, he looks at her. "Are …are you sure it's ok?" as she nods to give him consent, he nervously reaches his huge hands out, putting them on her flat tummy, sliding them up until he's massaging her amazingly soft and squishy breasts like a six-year-old playing with playdoh, as she moans quietly in pleasure. "I…. I'm not rubbing too hard, am I?" she shakes her head no, without saying anything, just lost in the moment. He looks at her, wondering if he can break out of his own comfort zone, "so…. you…. you've never…. seen a guy…?" she nervously blushes, "N…no…do….do you want me to see it?" He takes a deep breath and, nervously climbs out of the pool as she sees his huge member flopping out in full view, along with his muscular butt, as he stands there naked as the day he was born. "OH…Oh my… you look amazing…I…I guess I should get out too…" he takes a deep breath as she hops over the side of the pool, the butt from the mirror earlier comes into view, then she stands up to show off her amazing soft breasts and her bald vagina glistening from the sun on her wet skin.

He looks at his nude friend, "so…...do…do you like what you see?" turning blood red, she looks over his amazing frame "… oh…oh yes…can…can I…touch it?" he nervously shuffles closer to her as she reaches down, grasping her tiny hand around his now solid dick "oh…...oh my… are they all like this?" he stammers "uhhh…it…it's not always… hard… and they…..they're different sizes…" as she starts to move her hand back and forth slowly over his member. Gritting his teeth, he looks back at her "Do… do you…'explore?" as she suddenly blushes at his question "Only once…" and suddenly she feels his fingertips, rubbing against her wet hood, sending electric chills through her nude body, and it's more than the air sticking to them. As he tries to maintain eye contact with her, as she starts stroking him harder and faster, he slips two fingers in between her satin soft lips and runs his fingers in and out of her virgin hole as she bites her lip excitedly.

CHAPTER 6

"Sh…. should we…. go to your room?" without hesitation, she takes her nude friend by the hand and walks him down the hall to her bedroom where he was just hours before as she lays down on the bed, her right leg arched in the air with the other lying flat on the bed, as he looks over her fit body from years of volleyball. He slowly climbs up on the bed, lying beside her, he leans over and kisses her deeply, his huge hand rubbing her right breast slowly, his fingertip brushing her reddish nipple, causing it to poke out in excitement. Do…do you want me to eat you, or should we just…" But if you don't want to do anything like that, I won't force you to…." She looks up at him excitedly, "will I be your first too?" as he nods nervously. "Then yes, let's do it…I know you wouldn't hurt me…."

He slowly rolls over on top of his new friend as he reaches between their body and he slips his tip inside of her soft pussy, as her lips rub against his swollen dick, a chill goes through both of their bodies as he starts to push back and forth slowly. "Ooooh…. oh…that…. that feels good…" She twitches periodically at the feel of his member going back and forth inside her wet soft hole. Over the next fifteen minutes he starts plunging deeper and faster into her, thrusting his hips against hers as she gasps in approval each time his body slams into her. She pushes against the bed, causing them to roll as she ends on top for a bit, he slides his hands off her back, grasping a handful of her tight, athletic butt, pulling her into him.

They go back and forth, as she bounces around at his mercy, an unmistakable smile of pleasure on her face, she grabs the rails on the headboard to give her extra leverage as she plunges herself onto his amazing monster! "OH…OH MY GOSH…SO….SO GOOD…"

CHAPTER 7

After about an hour, he looks at her with a worried look......" I...I think I'm gonna blow.... should I pull out?" She looks at him thinking about the gravity of her decision, "If....if you aren't gonna disappear from my life forever after this, you can do it..." Suddenly, with her approval, he starts going almost like an extra gear until finally she feels his load of DNA explode into her as she howls with excitement! "OH... OH MY GOSH...THERE...THERE IT IS...!" Having blown his load inside the sweet girl, he falls back on the bed, letting the cool air from her fain blow over his sweaty torso as he listens to her try to collect her thoughts after their first experience. "Did....... did I do a good job? You were amazing..." blushing, she looks up at him "You were incredible too, such a gentleman, always checking to make sure I didn't feel forced or that you weren't hurting me...." She falls down beside him on the bed, wrapping her arm around is muscular torso as they look up at the ceiling thinking about the last hour. "Thank you for making my first time enjoyable." She says shyly "It was my pleasure; just glad it was everything we hoped it would be."

After about an hour, they get up and head back to the shower, this time together, before he gets dressed and heads back to his house. She sits in her bedroom in just her towel, trying to imagine how her life could get any better than its ben in the last 2 hours, anticipating getting to see her Prince Charming again soon.

Fan Support

CHAPTER 1

I t's a quiet day in a small town and Melissa is resting after a rough few days of college classes, even though she's not able to work with the pandemic going on. As she's doing some cleaning up around the house, she sees Brian, a cool disabled guy that comes to all their softball games games, struggling down the street. She looks again and realize he's been in some kind of accident and he's all scraped up as she goes out to meet him. "Hey! What the hell happened to you?!" looking over bruises and cuts on his face and arms "I…. I wrecked my chair down the street…" Holy crap man, get in here and let me get you cleaned up!" he blushes at the offer from his favorite gal on the softball team as he looks at her "Oh Uhh…I don't wanna get you in trouble with your folks or your…bf…" she scoffs… "Pshh… I live on my own and well, he'll just have to get over it!" He nervously follows her inside, watching as her hips sway in her softball shorts as she holds the door open and he goes on in, parking by the plaid couch. "Can I get you something to drink? Tylenol?" he takes a deep breath, "y…yeah Coke's fine…" she walks down the hall, coming back with Tylenol and a first aid kit as she looks him over. "Ok, this might hurt a bit…" as she dabs an alcohol swab over a cut on his forehead and scrapes on his arms. "Do…do I need to… take my shirt off?" as he looks nervously at her, she thinks for a minute before saying "Yeah, probably in case you have some other cuts…"

As he slowly slides his shirt off, wincing in pain, she tries not to gasp, seeing his chiseled but scarred torso. Finally, she snaps out of a mini-trance and sees a few cuts on his chest, which she dabs with more alcohol, feeling his rock-hard pecs through the cotton ball. "Does…. does that hurt?" she asks nervously. "No, it's not bad… trying not to show too much emotion, feeling her petite hands on his chest, she looks over again, making sure she didn't miss anything, when suddenly she sees some blood on his jeans.

CHAPTER 2

"Oh…you…your legs…are they cut too?" he swallows a lump in his throat, not sure if he's bleeding, but not sure if he can handle her checking him out." "Uh…I. I'm sure it's just blood drop left over from my chest…" as he blushes nervously. "Well, Uhh…. I…I should probably check things out, just to make sure you're safe…I mean…we're both adults, right?" as she bites her lip nervously.

He nervously looks around, "Uhh well…there's a lot of windows here… is there somewhere else we could do that?" starts to turn pink in embarrassment. "Uhh…we could go to the bathroom or my bedroom's got plenty of room…" he feels a chill go through his body as she says 'bedroom." "Well… whatever you think is best…" She helps push him down the hall across her thick carpet as they stop at the bathroom, but they can't fit his chair through the door. She takes a deep breath and pushes him on down the hall, as they enter a room covered in sports trophies and clothes thrown all on the floor, he tries not to notice a wadded-up thong by the corner of the bed. "S…sorry about the mess…" he looks back up at her "it…it's ok… so uhhh…. you want me to transfer over there?" as she nods nervously, he flops over, bouncing gently on the fluffy bed as she pulls his chair back out of the way. "So uhhh….t… take your pants off so I can check your legs…" as she tries to hide her emotions at the thought.

He looks up at her nervously, "can…can I make a confession?

I…I've never… in front of a beautiful lady…" as she blushes gently "aww it's ok… you're safe with me…" he looks around, seeing another small window in the room, wondering If anyone can see in. "I…I had a thought, but …I don't want to upset you…" as she looks at him puzzled, "what is it?" He swallows a lump in his throat, "well …uhhh…m… maybe I'd feel more comfy taking my jeans off… if uhhh…maybe you did it too?" he hangs head, hoping she doesn't kick him out and refuse to talk to him at anymore of the games.

CHAPTER 3

"Well, uhhh…I…I guess its…" all of a sudden, she drops her softball shorts, exposing a pair of lacy black bikinis as he can't help but stare." W…wow, you…you look amazing…" She blushes at him "thanks… so uhhh…do you need help?" he looks at her "oh…uhhh…right…" he nervously unbuttons the jeans, wiggling out of them and pulls them down to his knees as she sees his tighty whities, with a pretty nice sized bulge, as she makes eye contact with it her mouth flies open. "Wh…what's wrong…?" as he looks at her worried, she suddenly comes back to reality "Uhh nothing… just a few minor scrapes…lay back down…" as she helps take off his shoes and pulls his jeans off, she rubs alcohol on the small cuts, taking extra time to rub his legs, even though he can't use them, they feel nice." S….so uhhh… I never asked, what happened to you…sorry if that's intrusive…" he looks up at her, noticing her staring at his legs but thinking she's working on the cuts. "Well…, I was born not being able to use my legs…I can't feel my lower legs…" He looks up at her "can… can I ask a weird q? it may be none of my business, but uhhh… are you and Jim still going out?" blushing nervously, hoping he doesn't get too personal, as she looks up at him. "I…I think he's cheating on me, to be honest…" as she takes a deep breath, "well he's a jerk, to have such an awesome girl and if he is really messin' around…can… can I tell you something without upsetting you…?" she looks puzzled at him, "well I can't make too many promises but you're too nice of a guy to say something too mean... what is it?" the smile runs away from his face as he looks back at her "Well uhhh…. I kinda lied to you… I didn't wreck my chair…. Jim and his buddies came up behind me, making fun of me and they dumped me on the pavement and beat up on me…." As she hears his words, her face turns into an angry mess. "That nasty son of a…I've had it with him thinking he can hurt anyone he wants for no reason!"

He looks at her, "I'm, sorry if I caused a problem…" as she rubs his legs comfortingly, "no, it's not your fault he's an idiot! Have…. have you ever had a gf…?" He looks up at her with a bit of a mixed look "No, just friends that are girls…pretty sad right?" As she sits there looking over her friend, he can tell she's thinking about something. "Do you trust me Brian?" he looks at her puzzled "well yeah…...you've always been good to me…...why…?" She looks down at him, "Do…do you want me to teach you some things about girls?" he looks up at her nervously as she blushes slightly, "wh….wha?"

CHAPTER 4

I …I thought since Jim doesn't appreciate me like you do… I would help you out if you want… I won't force you to do anything…" he thinks about it a bit and looks at her "Well...I…I've never even been kissed…" as her eyes look into his eyes, feeling bad that such a sweet guy has been left to the side, she leans down and suddenly he feels her warm tongue swimming around in his mouth as he nervously tries to match her movements, hoping he's doing it right, as she pulls back as he watches her pull back "W... wow… I…I liked that...what...what else you want to teach me?" as he bites the corner of his lip "Have you ever seen a girl in a bikini?" he chuckles nervously "well yeah..." as she suddenly takes off her tee, sitting in front of him in her underwear. "See…. just like a bikini…" smiles shyly as he looks over her amazing muscular body, she watches his eyes. "Do you want to see my boobs?" As his eyes snap back up to her face "WH..Wha?!" she smiles shyly "…well…do you?" he can't get the words out, he just nods nervously as she reaches behind her back, and after a bit, she pulls the black top piece off as he suddenly comes face to face with her amazing breasts with brown dots on them. He starts to reach for them but puts his hands down; "C'mon… go ahead…they won't bite…" as she smiles, he nervously reaches up and cups her amazing breasts, squeezing them softly in his large, calloused hands. "Wow… they feel very nice..." she smiles at his enjoyment, "Run your finger over the brown spots…" as he does what she says, he sees them start to pop up like a flower blooming as he watches in amazement."

She looks into his brown eyes, "do you want me to take my bottoms off too?" as she smiles shyly "Y…you'd do that for me? as his eyes widen, she nods affirming his question, before he nods nervously, she stands up beside him on the bed as she slides her bottoms off, he sees the last of her tan muscular body, and a trimmed spot between her legs, as she watches him gloss over her body, he stops at the tuft of hair, looking puzzled. "Do...do you want to rub it too?" as her eyes sparkle. "He nervously reaches out as his fingertips squish into her trimmed pussy, he rubs it slowly, pushing his finger against it, feeling her soft skin against his fingertips, suddenly she squeaks in pleasure, and he jumps, causing his finger slips inside between her soft porcelain lips as he jumps nervously. "Oh…I'm sorry... did I hurt you?" as she chuckles "No…. not at all... in fact, will you do it again?" surprised by her words, he slips his finger back inside her wet hole, moving it back and forth some, before feeling her insides as she starts moaning.

CHAPTER 5

"Brian, do you trust me…?" he looks at her with a weird look and nods. "I'm gonna take your shorts off, are you ok with that?" Although his eyes widen in fear, he blushes and looks at her. "I…I guess it's only fair…." he slips his hand out of her wet pussy, and she leans down, putting her thumbs in his waist band as she pulls his shorts off, suddenly she gasps as she sees his solid 8 inches. "what? Is it bad?" he looks at her worried that she'll make fun of him to her friends. "N…no…you… you're bigger than Jim!" he springs up as he feels her hands wrap around his dick, starting to rub it slowly back and forth. "OH…OH MY…..That……. that feels so good…" as he bites his lip to stifle the urge to scream in pleasure!

"Do…do you want me to suck it?" as he looks up at her amazed at how the conversation has changed. "If… if you're gentle and won't hurt me…" She smiles innocently at his naivety, as she climbs up on the bed, hovering over his groin as she looks at it, taking it in her hand, she starts to wrap her tongue around the tip lightly. He gasps in pleasure as the feel of her tongue sends shockwaves through his body. "Oh…oh yes, it tastes so good…" he feels her start to put her mouth around his staff as she runs her lips back and forth over it, he can't help but massage her head through her brown hair, pushing her back and forth as she works over his throbbing cock.

After what feels like forever, she comes up and looks into his eyes. "Do…do you want to…you know…?" He bites his lip, looking at her "If…if you really want me to…would…..would I be your first too?" she nods at him nervously, as he looks up at her shocked, as she slowly climbs up on top of him, she grabs his member and slips it in between her soft wet lips, as she leans into him, pushing it deeper as she moans in pleasure as she pushes herself back and forth. "OH…OH YES…That…that feels so amazing!" As she starts grinding harder and faster, he gets more confidence, he slides his hands down her muscular back, he slowly rubs her butt, grabbing a big hand full of it as she bounces up and down on him.

She goes harder and faster, as she grabs his hands and puts them on her breasts as he squeezes them to keep them from bouncing out of control. For the next twenty minutes, she bounces harder and faster, grinding her soft skin into him until finally they feel a flood of his cream flood inside her as she yells in excitement. "OH... YES! OH MY GOSH THAT FELT SO GOOD! As she falls down on his torso, their sweaty bodies rubbing together, she kisses him deeply. "You…you were incredible…how does it feel to not be a virgin anymore?" as she smiles shyly. He blushes slightly "I…I can't tell you how much it means that you were willing to do this for me… you…you've always been my favorite on the team…" as he blushes again. They spend the next hour laying in the bed, talking about how much her ex would be pissed if he knew what was going on since he messed things up. From there on out, every time she sees him on campus, she invites him over and talks to her friends about her biggest fan and her best friend. After the semester, the two moved in together and they stayed in touch after graduating and moving a couple hours apart.

THE FRIENDLY SKIES

CHAPTER 1

Rushing around, Bobby finishes packing for his business trip to Orlando before his uber shows up. As he finishes everything, he runs out just as the uber is arriving and a guy named Johnny drops him off at the airport. He checks in at the desk, giving the nice lady all the needed information as she wishes him well and he continues thru security to the plane. As he walks on, a bubbly brunette gal looks at him "Hey there, thanks for flying with us today!" he greets her back, then puts his bag in the overhead as he grabs his aisle seat in the second row before slipping off for a nap.

Sometime later, he wakes up from his nap as the flight attendant that greeted him as he entered the plane, gives him a bag of Chex mix and offers him a drink. "Coke please," she pours the drink in the small cup of ice and hands it to him with a napkin with the company's logo on it as he takes it from her hand as she smiles and walks on through the aisle. Before she walks away, he notices her nametag that reads "Marie." Suddenly, he takes a gulp from his drink, taking a peek back through the plane, catching a peek of her amazing figure in the dark blue outfit.

As the flight lands and pulls up to the jetway, everyone rushes to grab their bags and stand in the aisle as they get things lined up as she opens the door for the mass exodus. As everyone streams out, she walks up to Bobby, "hey there, sorry I couldn't get you out quicker." He smiles at the wonderful young lady, "it's ok, this is my final so I'm in no rush…. where else are you off to today?" she gasps in exhaustion "We're here for the night, then we fly out tomorrow afternoon... such a long day!" "Well, I had a great experience as always!" As he gives her an exaggerated goofy smile, as he walks off the plane and through the terminal to pick up his rental car.

After picking up his car, he searches for his trip info to find the address for his hotel and inputs the info into his GPS for a short drive. He pulls up to a fancy hotel, gives his keys to the valet and walks to the check-in desk. As he's finishing up his check-in, he sees Marie coming through the doors. "Hey, what are you doin' here? I figured they put you guys up in a rat-hole closer to the airport" as he laughs. "Well, I had the option of getting my own hotel since we'll be leaving later in the day-why not splurge a little?" As she smiles shyly. "Well, uh…maybe we can get dinner somewhere if I can get away from this business meeting stuff?" she laughs briefly, "Yeah… here's my cell…" as she hands him a piece of paper with a number on it. "Ok, well I'm gonna go get settled in before my meeting…nice seeing you."

CHAPTER 2

Bobby gets registered for the conference goes back to his room, drops his stuff, and falls asleep for an hour, then gets up for a meeting then an after hours get together. Instead of going to the social function, he pulls out his phone and calls his newfound friend. "Hey, Marie, it's Bobby…...you wanna meet in the lobby and go find something to eat?" she nervously answers "…...yeah, that'd be fine, give me a half hour and I'll meet you down there." Later on, the elevator opens, and she comes out wearing a stunning purple dress that goes to mid-thigh as she walks over to where he's sitting in a fluffy chair wearing a button up shirt and dinner jacket with some khakis. "Wow… you look great… definitely not airline issue dress." As he blushes nervously. "So uhhh, what kinda food do you like?" as he watches her contemplating "Well, I like a bit of everything, but how about some Italian?"

He gets up and they walk to the door as he holds the door open for her then hails the hotel shuttle. "Hey… can you take us to a nice Italian restaurant close by?" "Sure can boss," the driver says affirmingly. The van pulls up to a nice-looking place as he tips the driver a few bucks and helps her out of the van, holding the door as she goes in the restaurant and looking around.

They are seated by the waiter as they look over the menu full of delectable delights and they finally order. "So, you know what I do, what about you?" as she looks at him over the small candle in the middle of their table. "Well, I work with an organization that partners with our local children's hospital." Her eyes sparkle as his mission is so heartwarming, even if he isn't directly involved with the patients. "That's amazing, I wish I could know that what I did made a difference in people's lives!' he looks at her face glowing in the candlelight. "Well, we've been thinking about talking to the airlines about helping with a program we have that's like Make-a-wish, maybe you'll get to help us soon."

Soon the waiter walks up with the most amazing smelling and looking food that either of them have seen in a long time. Donning their napkins, they dig into their food as she groans in approval. "oh, my goodness this is so good!"

CHAPTER 3

After a couple hours of amazing food and great conversation, he looks at her "well, I guess we should get outta here…" He pays the bill as she gives him a stern look for not, at least, splitting the bill. "You didn't have to do that ya know! At least let me leave a tip…" Soon, the shuttle van comes around the corner and picks them up and takes them back to the hotel.

"Hey uhhh…you…you wanna come upstairs for a drink? I don't know what time you have to be back at the airport tomorrow…" She looks at her companion, "Sure, I figure a short visit wouldn't hurt, since you're offering…" He takes her by the arm as they ride the elevator up and he opens the door to a sprawling room with clothes pushed in one corner. She sits on the bed as he pours a couple drinks and hands one to her, noticing she is stretching her neck back and forth. "You ok?" he asks with a concerned look. "Well, some of us don't get to sleep during a two-hour flight while someone serves our every whim….my neck and shoulders are killin' me…" he smiles at her comment about the services, taking it in jest." He slowly walks over and climbs up on the bed as he starts working her shoulders, digging his thumbs into her neck gently. He runs his hands up and lightly starts to give her a scalp massage as his hands come back down her neck and out to her shoulders as he rubs them thoroughly, but not too hard. "Oh…… oh my goodness that feels good…" she says, almost lost in the moment. "Shh…relax…." as he puts his huge hands on the middle of her back, running his palms back and forth, like kneading bread, first to the left then right. Next, he rolls his fists over her back gently, then he taps all over it gently like rain falling on the roof in the spring as she lets a slight moan of appreciation escape. "Do… do you trust me to unzip the dress so I can get to your back easier?" she pauses for a moment, then slowly reaches around unzips the dress down to her waist, he sees her muscles from constantly pushing drink cards and tossing luggage around all day, covered with a black bra strap.

He goes back up, starting at her neck again, and out to the shoulders, as he rubs the shoulders, the dress slips gently off her shoulders. Nervously, he grabs the dress and pulls it back up on her shoulders. "S…sorry…" suddenly, without hesitation, she grabs the dress again, pulling the dress off the shoulders, holding it in a bunch in front of her leaving her back exposed completely for his magical touch. "It…

it's ok... I trust you..." After a bit of a bit of a pause, he puts his thumbs in the small of her back, just above the waistline of the dress, running them up her spine, stopping at the bra strap, going above it, and continuing, up and down a couple times as she groans in approval. "Mm mm.... where.... where did you learn this?" As he smiles to himself, he whispers

"I wasn't always in the hospital business."

CHAPTER 4

S he can't take the feeling anymore, as she slowly scoots up. "Hold…...hold on…" Suddenly she stands up, sliding the dress to the floor, he sees her in the lacy black bra and a matching thong as he bites his lip as she lays down. After he swallows a lump in his throat at the sight of her body, he kneels down beside her, as he feels a knot on her back, he pushes around on it thoroughly. "Ooh, there's a tough one…would…would you be ok if I straddled your back to get more pressure on that knot?" She suddenly smiles to herself and looks back towards him "I…...I guess so," wondering if he believes that she is nervous about him doing it, he suddenly climbs over on her muscular back, kicking his leg over to the side, sitting on the small of her back.

He works on the knot to where he feels like he got it broken down and goes over her back again. He leans down and whispers in her ear "Did…. did I forget anything?" Suddenly she leans her head to the side, just one thing…." As he thinks about the procedure, what could he have possibly forgotten? Suddenly, she rolls over underneath him as she is now staring up into his sapphire blue eyes. "Do…do you like what I see?" as she blushes up at him. "You…you look amazing…" Without a word, he leans down and kisses her deeply as she feels his huge hand sliding up her thin torso and suddenly, he starts massaging her breast slowly through the material as she moans silently. He sits up and pulls his khakis down, exposing his boxers with a nice sized bulge coming into view as he leans back down on top of her as she takes the bra off and her amazing D cups flop out into full view.

He slowly kisses her deeply again, but this time, he runs his tongue down her neck and before she knows what is going on, he starts licking and sucking on her soft mounds as he tugs each of her pink nips with his teeth as she lets out a noise in pleasure to his touch. "OH…Oh my…. that tickles…..." As she laughs at the feeling of his mouth on her chest, she slowly reaches her small hand down and slips it in his boxers, grabbing his amazingly large member, running her hand over it slowly as he grits his teeth. "Oh…oh...you found my little friend I see.... "As his eyes roll back in his head at the feeling of her hand stroking him through his boxers, he slowly slides his hand down her flat tummy to return the favor, slipping his large hand inside her damp panties, gently rubbing her hood with two fingers, as her mound squishes under his fingers.

CHAPTER 5

He watches a look of euphoria wash over her face as he slowly slips the two fingers inside her pussy, her juices sticking to his fingers as he traces her insides slowly. As he slowly moves the fingers back and forth inside her, she starts gasping in pleasure, before he pulls them out and he gently pulls her silk thong down to her knees, exposing her thin patch of trimmed hair. She bites her lip in ecstasy as she fumbles with his boxers, trying to get them down as he reaches back, pulling them down to his knees as she sees his rock hoard dick staring at her.

"Oh...oh wow...it looks incredible..." as she reaches out and starts to stroke him again, fondling his sack gently, he starts to stand up in front of the bed, she looks at his member as she leans in, kissing his rock-hard stomach before grabbing his throbbing cock and running her tongue across the tip of it slowly. He grabs her shoulders for support as his knees start to buckle at her touch, as she leans in, slipping it in her mouth, her warm breath causing chills through his body as she rubs his butt with her small hands while her lips go back and forth over him.

CHAPTER 6

After what feels like forever, he has to pull out of her, so he doesn't blow his load early, as she looks up at him disappointed. "It's my turn now..." as he playfully tosses her back in the bed, he runs his strong hands up her muscular tan legs, hovering over her trimmed mound before he leans in and slowly traces a circle with his tongue, her body quivering at his touch. "OOOH…Oh that…. that tickles…" He slowly flicks his tongue up and down her hood, running the length of her velvety lips before penetrating her barrier, tasting her fluid on his tongue as he explores her insides. "Ahh…ooh… oh my…" She can't get a full sentence out from the feel of his touch, all she can do is to massage his head through his dark hair.

As he continues to dig into her, he slides his hands under her nude body, grasping her butt to pull his tongue deeper as he massages her from both sides as she gasps in pleasure above him, feeling like he's gonna drill all the way through her body. As her body almost shakes with excitement, she finally yells out loud, "OMG Take me now!" Hearing her cues, he slowly pulls out of her soaked trimmed pussy, he slides up her nude body with his tongue, kissing her deeply so she can taste her own fluid on his tongue as he slowly slips his tip inside her with a gentle push.

As she feels him enter her, she slowly starts pushing her hips off the bed, meeting his pulsing member as they start merging back and forth, both bodies swarming with tingles from the touch of the other.

After about 5 minutes, she wiggles around so that they roll over on the bed, with her now mounted on top of him, slamming into his rock-hard member from above like a kid with a pogo stick, and her breasts bouncing out of control! "OH…OH YES… OH MY GOSH…." As he puts his hands on her hips to keep her from falling backward as she arches her back in pleasure as their bodies slap against each other during the passionate hot sex.

CHAPTER 7

As he grabs the headboard for support to keep slamming back and forth, he finally looks into her green eyes, "Oh...

oh my.... I...I think I'm about to...sh.....should I pull out?" Not able to get any words out, she keeps on going with a quick nod as he seems to go into a warp-speed, bouncing her up and down so hard, she feels like she's going to fly off! Finally, with one final thrust, she feels his mess explode inside her, feeling like a firecracker exploding inside her body as she tingles all over! "OH! OH YESS! Ahh..... wow..." as he falls into his chest with an exhale. "Was it as good for you as it was for me?!" she looks at him with a look of exasperation on her face, hair draped all across her face. "You were incredible!" She slowly lays down on his sweaty torso, feeling his heart still pounding from their recent workout as he kisses her head gently. "I'm glad you enjoyed it to..."

CHAPTER 8

As they lay there for a while, talking about how they could be able to spend more time together, she looks at her watch. "Well, I guess I should go back to my room and get some sleep…I had a wonderful night." With a slightly disappointed, but understanding look on his face, he watches as she pulls the cover away and walks around the room naked to grab her things and get dressed enough to not make it obvious what she's been doing.

She takes one last look at him, wishing she could stay. "Will you call me when you get home from your meetings?" he smiles at her as she starts to walk over to the bed, "Well of course!" as he kisses her deeply one last time, watching as she walks out the door. He sits there thinking about how great his night was, then slowly walks to the door. He locks it, with a pause, half hoping she would knock again, but walks back to the bed and goes to sleep to get ready for a day full of meetings.

HEALING HANDS

CHAPTER 1

"Code 3, MVA incoming…3 minutes!" the announcement rings through the hospital as the people run frantically through the ER getting ready for the next great tragedy to take care of through the night. Faith watches as they bring yet another mangled patient through the doors, spouting off vitals and diagnostic information. She'd been working her shift for 6 hours, taking vitals and making sure her patients are comfortable and well taken care of while they wait on the next doctor on call, but now it's time for her to get her lunchbreak before the next wave hits.

After she grabs a bite to eat, she goes back to the hospital to finish her shift out before getting a few days off. When she comes back two days later, she walks on the floor to look at the board and see that she will be taking care of an accident victim in room #3 today. She walks in, introducing herself to a sweet looking young man, looking to be in his mid-twenties as she starts taking some vitals. "Are you feeling any better today, Mike?" as he sighs with exasperation, "I mean…I guess…things could probably be a lot worse…" suddenly he pulls the sheet back, and she notices that they had to take his legs, which she didn't know about since she didn't get to read his chart before morning vitals. "Well, hey…you're still alive, and you didn't mess up that cute face of yours." She gives him a shy smile as she looks at his scraped-up face, finishing up taking his BP and taking notes. "Do you need anything else?" as she starts to walk away, she can see the disappointment leave his face ever so slightly. "No…I guess I'm ok for now, just waiting on some breakfast," as he gives her a forced smile. "I just hope it's not the 'eggs'." As he gives her air quotes, she chuckles. "Hey… not all the food's that bad…I'll be back in later honey."

CHAPTER 2

Early the next week, she comes back in to check on her newfound friend, happy that he keeps progressing from an accident that should've probably killed him. "Hey! How's our hero doin' today?" as he chuckles at her over-enthusiasm, "nice to see you too Nurse Ratched..." as he gives her a cheesy smile. "Well, the doc says I should only be another week or two, then I need to find somewhere to stay till I learn to use my prosthetics." She checks on his medicines and makes some more notes. "I'll be in to change your medicine in an hour or so..." as she walks out the door, he suddenly notices her hips swaying in her scrubs as she walks out and pulls the door mostly closed.

When she comes back later, she changes the big bag of saline and hooks up a new bag of medicine. "There....good to go for a while! Do you need anything else?" he looks down a bit "Can.... can you close the door for a second?" she gives him a weird look, and after some hesitation, she goes over and closes the door. "Can...Can I ask you a personal question?" as she blushes at him, "well uhhh... I don't think that'd be proper...but uhhh...... what's on your mind?" not sure what to expect from her friend's new quandary. "Do......do you have a boyfriend?" as she looks nervously at him, he realizes how his question sounded. "Oh uhhh.... not that.... I mean uhhh......I lost my girlfriend in the wreck. I haven't been with a girl since before the wreck. I...I don't want to get you in trouble but will...will you...grab it?" as he grits his teeth, she gets a mortified look on her face. "I...I can't! I'd get fired and have my license taken away... you should know I can't do anything like that!" as she walks out of the room, embarrassed that he'd ask such a question!

CHAPTER 3

A few hours later, she comes back in for his vitals check, as she gives him a stern look. "Hey…I'm….I'm sorry for what I said earlier…. I know it'd turn out bad, but I…. I wouldn't tell anyone if anything happened…" she looks over his beat-up body, the scars on his face healing nicely as she looks at him slightly embarrassed, "well, let's look over these dressings and make sure they're ok." She gently pulls the curtain back to give them some privacy, as she pulls the blanket down and lifts his gown to see his stubs where his legs used to be, but suddenly she notices his surprisingly large member as she bites her lip, looking up at him, as he realizes she took a look at it. She looks back and forth a bit, and finally she exhales and gives him the "shhh" signal, as she slowly puts on her gloves, she reaches between his stubs and wraps her tiny hand around his member gently as she starts to rub her hand back and forth over it slowly. "Ohhh…oh that feels good…" he whispers, as she blushes harder, slowly stroking it harder, brushing her gloved hand over the tip slowly." Trying to fake sounding professional, since no one could see past the curtain if they walked in the door. "Does…does it hurt there?" as she winks nervously at him, he tries to build up the calmness to give her a convincing "No…no it's fine…." after a bit more foreplay, she snaps off her gloves overly loud in case someone was walking by the cracked door, as she leans over, she grabs his scarred-up hands and places them nervously on her soft breasts through her scrubs with a shy wink. "Thank you, nurse…that should help me feel better for a while…" he speaks louder than normal, as he gives her a wink as he nervously massages her soft breasts through the durable material of her scrubs as she puts him back together and pulls the curtain back and walks back to the station."

CHAPTER 4

Over the next week or two, she keeps coming by to check on him, but keeps it mostly professional, other than sneaking a quick peck, or smiling if she's beside his bed and his hand accidently rubs against her thin butt. "So, have they said anything about you getting out yet?" she looks at him pensively. "Well, PT says I'm doing well, but I need to find a place I can live." She looks at him shyly and whispers "My apartment is one floor, and I have a spare room…. I could have a friend of mine pick you up and take you there till I get off work…" He looks up at her with a look to say, "are you sure?" as she nods at him assuredly. A few days later, she's doing her rotations and she walks past his room, seeing the doctors talking to him, as she sees her friend Lisa in his room, acting as his guardian to be released to him. An hour later, he rolls out in a wheelchair with Lisa following, carrying his stuff as he pulls up to the nurse's station.

"Hey Faith, this is my friend Lisa……she's gonna help me get settled for a few days." She smiles at him and Lisa, trying not to let on that there's something going on, she reaches out to shake Lisa's hand. "Good luck honey, he's been a rock star on the floor here. Hope you'll take good care of him," as she gives Lisa a wink. "Oh yeah… we'll make sure he's well taken care of." As she gives Faith and all the nurses a smile, they go on down the hall and get in the elevator to head to Faith's house.

They get to Faith's tiny apartment and she takes the key that Faith gave her the day before as he rolls in, Lisa takes him to the spare room and help him get stuff put in the drawers. "Get a rest and when you build up your strength, we can go to your house and get the rest of your stuff." He nods, "thanks for helping out…I bet you think we're crazy…" he nervously smiles as she looks at him. "Hey, Faith and I have been friends since junior high, I'm just glad she finally found a sweet guy that will treat her right."

CHAPTER 5

Lisa lets herself out, as Mike looks around the house, trying to get the lay of the place in his head, he grabs a coke out of the fridge and goes to the living room to watch some tv. A few hours later, he hears the door and Faith comes in from another long day at the hospital and gives him a peck on the lips. "Hey honey, I hope you got yourself settled?" he smiles, "yeah, glad the plan worked out and you didn't get in any trouble for helping me out." She sits down beside him on the couch with a glass of water, her scrubs top pooching out some, showing some of the tee underneath it as he looks at her shyly. "You up for a conversation, or you too tired?" as he gives her a sheepish look, without even thinking, she nervously grabs her new special friend, sitting him on her lap, she leans over and kisses him deeply, now that she doesn't have to hold back. As she finishes up the kiss, he grabs the tail of her scrubs top and pulls it off with her help leaving an old tee with a floral design. He looks at it as she nods, he grabs it slowly and lifts it off, showing off her amazing, tanned torso with a bustling pink Victoria Secrets bra.

Suddenly he puts his large, scarred hands on her shapely tummy, tracing his finger up her abs to the material, as he slowly massages them gently, before pulling the bra down as her tanned D cups drop out of the cups onto his hand with her puffy pink nipples staring at him. He slowly rubs them, just as he did before, but now, with nothing in between their skin-to-skin contact, and no one to yell at them if they got caught." Mmm…your hands feel amazing…do you like them?" he smiles at her, "they're perfect, just like you…..." After a bit, she puts him to the side as she stands in front of the couch, doing a sexy little dance, she shimmies out of the scrubs, showing off a lacy thong, showing off some extra sultry moves in front of him before shaking her butt in front of him jokingly. She jumps as she feels his hands grab her thighs, working their way up, he slowly rubs his hands all over her muscular butt, grasping each cheek gently, feeling the muscle she's built up from running the hospital halls for the last couple years.

CHAPTER 6

She sits beside him, kissing him again deeply, "Did you and your girlfriend ever...do things?" He looks up her with a twinge in his eyes, thinking about her memory, but knowing she'd be happy that he found someone else special. "Some, but not a lot..." did you have something in mind?" She picks him up and helps him into his wheelchair as she leads him down the hall to a messy bedroom as he hops out of the chair and swings himself along the floor, until she helps him up onto the bed. She slowly pulls his shorts off, then his tee, leaving him totally nude as she removes her thong, joining him on the bed as he looks over her amazing, fit body. "Wow...you look amazing, as he looks over her perky breasts down to her bald pussy. He slides up to her as he starts to lick her neck playfully, running it down her torso, over her puffy pink nips and doing a circle around her bellybutton, tugging on her belly ring playfully as he starts to rub her bald pussy slowly, hearing her moan slowly at his touch.

He looks up at her nervously, "Do...do you......rub yourself?" she looks at him blushing, "On..........only once..." as she bites her lip, he starts to rub up and down on her soft mound as it squishes against his touch as his finger traces over her split, rubbing it so softly that his fingers don't split her lips apart. Finally, he gets a boost of confidence as his strong finger slips between her babysoft lips, exploring her insides as her wet juices stick to his finger as it moves around inside her. Feeling overcome with excitement, she reaches out and grabs his now solid member again, just like the time in the hospital, but this time no one to tell them "no," she starts jerking it harder than she did the first time. "OH...oh wow... someone...someone's excited!" he exclaims as his eyes perk up at the feeling of her extra vigor with their new private arrangement solidified.

She looks down at him as they rub each other, "have you ever...tasted a woman?" he blushes, "n...no...do you want to be my first?" She smiles at him and nods as she lays down, spreading her legs out, as he bounces up between her legs nervously, he bends down and hovers over her glistening mound as his breath causes chill bumps of excitement to form. Suddenly, as she looks at the pattern of the stucco ceiling, she tenses up as she feels his tongue slip inside her, as he tries to get used to the taste of her sticky fluid. "Ohhh...oh yes... that feels amazing..." Hoping he's doing it right, hie shifts his tongue around inside her, as she continues to moan and make guttural noises of approval. As he slips his hands under her nude body to massage her muscular backside, she can't help but reach down and massage his head through his dark hair, pushing him slightly back and forth into her body as the impulses shoot through her body. "Oh… oh yes...

taste me babe…"

CHAPTER 7

F ive minutes later, he comes out from between her legs and looks at her. "Do you want to…you know….?" Blushing, she looks at him "I…. if you want to…we don't have to rush it." As he gives her a hand motion to lay down, he nervously flops around, climbing up on top of her, he reaches down and slowly slips the tip of his large member inside her has she gasps at her lips being spread apart. As he starts to push it inside her and pulling out slowly, he tries to make a rhythm that won't hurt her but will be enjoyable as she starts to shutter slightly, in pleasure. "Oooh…oh that feels good…." She slowly pushes her hips off the bed periodically, meeting his member against her bald pussy as their skin starts smacking together as they meet with each thrust. "Oh my gosh, this feels so good…are you sure you've never done this…" Working his hardest to make a good first impression, he keeps thrusting harder and faster. "N…no….you're really my first…." As his stubs balance on her muscular thighs, both quivering with excitement, she grabs his strong but scarred backside as she pulls him into her, making each thrust of his pelvis go even deeper inside her as she shrieks with approval.

CHAPTER 8

As they go on for the next ten minutes, both breathing heavily, sweating, and making weird noises of approval, he looks down at her, "I…...I think it's that time…should I pull out?" he looks up at him excitedly as her eyes sparkle in anticipation. "I…will leave it up to you…...if you want to you can, but if you blow your load in me, I won't be disappointed." He pushes back and forth, trying to decide what to before deciding that she's been nothing but amazing and probably saved his life, he goes into a different level. He bounces up and down on her, getting what leverage he can without his legs to drive into her, when suddenly he feels her squirt her fluid onto his swollen member just below his load explodes into her like someone running over a fire hydrant as she screams in pleasure. "OH MY, THAT WAS AMAZING!" as her head falls back onto the sweaty pillow, he slowly leans down, inches from her exasperated face. "You….….. you were amazing…I hope I did a good job for our first." Her smile of approval beams up at him. "Yes….…. you were incredible, and always nothing but a gentleman…" as she kisses him deeply.

They lay there for a few hours, both thinking about how their lives have changed for the better over the last month, they discuss the thought of living together, and maybe something

more down the line. Finally, she crawls out of the bed and throws on a ratty tee, looking at him. "Where are you going?" as he looks a bit puzzled. "Well, I figured I would make an amazing meal for the most special guy I've ever met….and I figure you wouldn't mind some real food, since I'm the only thing you've eaten that wasn't nasty ol' hospital food." As she gives him a goofy smile at her comparison, he chuckles and falls back on the bed, laying there looking up at the ceiling.

Printed in the United States
by Baker & Taylor Publisher Services